My Spiritual Journal of Guided Meditations

Paige

My Spiritual Journal of Guided Meditations

Paige

Serene Escapes & Healing
Westminster, CO

My Spiritual Journal of Guided Meditations

Serene Escapes & Healing
Paige

Serene Escapes & Healing
8774 Yates Dr. #305B Westminster CO 80031
SereneEscapesHealing@gmail.com

Cover Credit: Whitney Wiedner, Graphic/Web Designer
                  Whitney@wlwgd.com
                  www.wlwgd.com

Editor Credit: Helena Mariposa
                  HelenaMariposa@comcast.net

Interior Credit: Interior layout by Kerrie Lian, under contract with
                  Karen Saunders & Associates
                  www.KarenSaundersAssoc.com

Author: Tiffany Paige Land
                  8774 Yates Dr. #305B Westminster CO 80031
                  www.MetaphysicalMommies.com
                  www.SereneEscapesHealing.com

Printed in the United States of America

September 2015

ISBN: 978-0-692-45398-8
LCCN: 2015911323

Disclaimer: The material in the book cannot substitute for professional advice; further, the author is not liable if the reader relies on the material and is financially damaged in some way, and if it is a biography, a statement about the recollection of stories shared are recalled to the best of the author's knowledge, etc.

Contents

Gratitude

I would first like to express my gratitude for all the support and creativity that Spirit has showered upon me. I feel extremely blessed to be able to share the gifts I have received. Next I want to thank the love of my life Justin and my pack of munchkins for all their unyielding support and patience as I balanced motherhood, partnership, and my pursuit of the many things that led me forward on my soul journey path.

I also want to thank my mom and those on the East Coast who supported her and made it possible for her to spend months at a time with us in Colorado. This not only gave her a chance to enjoy her amazing grandchildren, but it also gave me time to meet the deadlines involved in the creation of this book.

And last, but definitely not least, I want to thank all the wonderful mentors, business partners, and friends who made this project possible with their creative touches and professional guidance. In particular, I would like to acknowledge a few of the special people who helped bring this project to life.

Kim Fanelli, my friend and mentor, for all her creative ideas, life coaching, motivation, encouragement, and love. Check her out at www.TheLifePathLady.com located in Colorado.

Karen Saunders for her relentless support of my many questions during the process of completing this project. She works with and contracts some of the best professionals in the self-publishing industry. Check her out at www.KarenSaundersAssoc.com located in Colorado.

Whitney Wiedner for graphics and book cover design. She is an awesome artist from Texas. Check her out at Whitney@wlwgd.com or www.wlwgd.com.

Gus Hoffman, with Cherry Sound Records, for the creative audio work that brought my book to life. Contact him at Gustav@CherrySoundRecords.com or Gustavoffman@gmail.com. He is located in Colorado.

Paula Ruelas for the voice-over work in the audio production of my book. She is located in Colorado and can be contacted at PCRuelas@comcast.net.

Justin Windham for his unyielding love, support, and business knowledge that guided me in creating my company Serene Escapes & Healing in order to publish this book. Contact him at www.DiscountSolo401K.com.

I have met so many amazing people along the path of my soul journey thus far and cannot wait for what lies ahead. I am forever grateful for the knowledge they imparted and for the cheering squad they all became as they witnessed me develop into the person I was truly meant to be.

Now to begin . . .
My Spiritual Journal of Guided Meditations

Introduction

In my constant searching for a closer connection to Spirit and clearer understanding of spirituality, I was blessed to meet some wonderful mentors who imparted wisdom and helped me succeed in finding my place in the metaphysical world. I am overwhelmingly grateful for their guidance, especially for the ways they have directed me in exploring meditation and mindfulness. Through a lot of soul searching and spiritual exploration, I have discovered the true meaning of meditation for me personally. I have seen the level of consciousness rise in my daily life the more I have striven to connect to the Divine Source.

For most people meditation is a very solitary, disciplined, and somewhat challenging practice. I struggled for years with the idea of quieting my mind. I tried every scenario. I attempted every recommendation offered in the many books I read on the importance of meditation. But as usual I realized I was not like the norm. I needed something more uniquely designed for me. That's when I started experimenting with guided meditations.

Over time, as I completed meditations, I noticed that I was able to more quickly quiet my mind and connect with higher levels of consciousness and Spirit. But something was still missing. It was as though each guided meditation fell short of its full potential. At the end of a meditation, I felt the need to continue and go deeper into the meditative state.

So after several months of following different guided meditations, I began to push past this point and drifted longer and further into my own space each time the meditation was over. I would wake from the meditation and write about all that I saw. I could almost always connect messages I received to current situations in my life. These messages helped with areas that needed healing and provided guidance in my soul journey. I even started to recall past life events and made connections to things in nature that I had always been attracted to but didn't understand why.

One day I looked at my beat-up notebook with pages of scribbled notes and realized that throughout the months of finding my own way in the world of meditation, I had unintentionally created a journal of all the details of my journeys. I reread my notes and discovered I had connected with Spirit guides, identified Spirit animals, discovered the rebirthing power of flowers, and grounding abilities of trees. I had also received enlightenment on rocks/crystals, energy work, and soul connections to the other side.

I was so overwhelmed with gratitude that, with severe determination on my part and divine intervention from Spirit, I was able to absorb all of this sacred knowledge from the comfort of my own home. Of course, I also have had assistance from other sources. I have taken numerous metaphysical classes. I have read a ton of books and researched the meaning of anything that seemed intuitively important. Through Reiki certifications and practice, I have discovered the healing abilities of energy and have become more attuned to the energy around me. But despite this outside help, the real lessons and journey started inside.

I realized, reflecting back on the past few years of my metaphysical work, that without my journal to remind me of all the details discovered in each meditation and daily experiences, I would not have been able to remember everything or cherish its validity in my life. So I decided to share my love for guided meditations and passion for the spiritual world by creating this book so others can also create their own soul journal. The information you will receive on these guided journeys will bring awareness of spiritual beings and energies that are waiting to help you achieve evolvement if only you ask and remain open for guidance.

This book will be a journal in which you collect basic spiritual information that is personal to you, in order to reflect back on it and learn. It will be a very sacred experience, if you take the time to really absorb the energy shared in the meditations and truly open yourself to the guides and the other metaphysical beings who are willing to help you in your journey. You will notice you develop stronger connections to Mother Earth and nature as well as more awareness to energy and its effect on your daily life.

Throughout the meditations, there may be information you do not immediately understand, like chakras, rock/crystal energy, and color connections to Spirit. I would even venture to say that parts of the book may stretch your personal beliefs regarding the afterlife and connections with spiritual entities. Despite any limiting beliefs you may have prior to completing this journal, trust me when I tell you that when you are finished, you will feel a deeper connection to the Divine Source of life, whatever or whoever that is to you. It will be especially helpful if you determine in the beginning to stay open-minded to anything that presents itself to you through each meditation. Imagination is a powerful tool that is often taken for granted as pure make-believe, but if you could just allow yourself to create a paradigm shift about imagination you will find it is one of Spirit's most potent forms of communication. When you let go of judgment and release the limiting ideas around imagination, you will trust that what is shown or shared with you during meditation has a place of meaning in your journey. If it doesn't appear to apply in the moment, know that there will be a time or situation where its application becomes obvious.

With your journal you will always be able to reflect back and find its significance. Each meditation will create vivid memories, leaving you with life tools to aid in tackling daily situations. By connecting with guides, you will feel supported and know who to call upon for help.

The meditations in this book will assist in helping you connect with your higher self. They will bring greater control over your personal energy and path during a time when the world seems like anything but under control. By working with energy, you will feel empowered to control your own space and recognize when other people or situations are affecting you negatively. With a stronger understanding of your connection to nature, you will feel more grounded and prepared to take on difficulties and conquer fears.

Enlightenment in so many areas will come from embracing the information in this book, listening to what the meditations ask of you, and truly taking the time to document what you receive in your own unique journaling format. You will understand your purpose more clearly and walk away healed and empowered to change yourself and share that peace with others. You will find that you end this book with a stronger connection to nature, spirituality, and self-worth. You will realize that closeness with Spirit, whether that be God, Mother Earth, pure science, or pure energy, is what we are here for.

My hope is this journal will awaken something in you that you will feel compelled to share with others. Our soul journey is enhanced through relationship and guiding each other. As we share and evolve through life experiences with others, we discover the meaning of compassion, love, life, and enlightenment. Increased compassion, love, and enlightenment will lead us to want to help others. In order to truly help others, we must understand and heal ourselves first. This book is my way of helping you begin that process.

I am so excited to share the magic and beauty you will find within the pages of this book. I love the creativity and bravery involved in choosing to embark on guided meditations and the commitment it takes to document your journey in the pages of this journal. I applaud you for buying this book, and I am eager to see the difference it makes in the universe as it affects one life at a time starting with you.

Why Meditate?

Meditation is one way to gain access to the still, small voice that is your true self. When you are able to connect to that voice, you will be amazed by the insightful answers it gives to your most pressing questions of life, love, and purpose. With daily meditation you train yourself to remain calm and collected in difficult situations. You also gain access to higher realms of the divine, which is not only inspirational but also healing. Meditation is a commitment that if pursued will turn into a life choice that becomes second nature to you.

A meditative state can be experienced through traditional formats or achieved through mindfulness of your surroundings in daily life. I have found some of my deepest, most cherished experiences have occurred in nature on a hike or sometimes even while driving in rush hour traffic. A place of meditation can be anywhere that is conducive to freeing your mind from daily worries and future fears. It does take time and practice to be able to hear the still, small voice. I found guided meditations to be a doorway to other forms of meditation, which helped make it more natural for me to achieve the meditative state anywhere.

Experiment with ways to quiet your voice as you sit back and relax with this book of guided meditations. Remember, it is okay to fall asleep during a guided meditation. Subconsciously you will still absorb the information being shared, and it will reveal itself to you again when needed. Do not judge yourself or try to perfectly answer each question asked in the meditations. Consider this journal your piece of artwork for this part of your life journey. Be creative and make it personal to you. I encourage you to not only use words when documenting what you receive, but also draw pictures and decorate with color. Have fun, listen, be patient, and know that if you have to repeat meditations more than once to feel connected, that is normal. Relax in a space of absolute safety from judgment or criticism, and open your mind to the beauty of the spiritual plane.

Meditations

Stone Energizing Chakra Clearing Meditation

Close your eyes and find a comfortable position. You may sit up with your feet flat on the floor or lie down. Whichever you prefer is great.

We are going to start by taking three deep breaths. Okay, let's begin.

Here we go, first breath. Inhale, hold, one . . . two . . . three . . . now exhale. Notice your face and shoulders start to relax.

Okay, again, inhale, hold, one . . . two . . . three . . . now exhale. Notice your legs and arms start to relax, and then your entire body.

One more time, inhale, hold, one . . . two . . . three . . . now exhale. The stresses of your day are melting away. You are now ready for the journey.

Imagine you are sitting with your legs crossed on an inviting, quiet beach. Lying next to you is a unique basket woven from native sea grass. It is just you and your basket on this deserted beach and you are completely at ease. Feel the sand beneath you. Hear the waves splashing against the shore. Feel the mist of the ocean blowing against your face. Look out into the vast open water and absorb the energy around you. Close your eyes and smile as you feel the warmth of the sun's glow. Listen quietly and don't forget that you are alone on the beach, completely in control of your personal feelings and emotions. As you sit and watch the waves flowing inland, you can feel the strength, energy, and life it possesses radiating up from the sand. As you focus on this power, you notice it begins to intensify. With each pounding wave, the vibration of life grows stronger and stronger. Then suddenly, stones begin popping up from beneath the sand. The stones are beautiful hues of white, purple/indigo, blue, pink, green, yellow, orange, and red. They are different in texture and size. The colors are vibrant like nothing you have seen before. Your eyes are drawn to specific stones. As you are attracted to these stones, collect them and place each one into your basket. Notice any specific characteristics that speak to you. Take a moment with each one to feel the energy it exudes. Connect with each stone individually before placing it in your basket. Make sure you collect stones of each color.

Good.

Now, sit back down, with your legs crossed, and place your basket in front of you. As I call out the color of a stone, I would like you to pick up that specific stone and listen to my instructions.

First, we will start with your red stone. This stone represents your base/root chakra. As you pick up your stone and place it between your legs, envision the red color shining as bright as possible, projecting an extreme red force of light towards the ocean in front of you. Our soul's life force and passions are rooted in this area. This chakra establishes the deepest connections with your physical body, your environment, and the earth. It is your instinctual and survival center that aids in keeping you grounded. It must remain clear, strong, and pure for overall physical well-being. Notice now how your red light appears. If it is not bright and powerful, ask Spirit to help clear and heal this area for you. Concentrate and pull from the energy of your red stone until you feel the light is as it should be. Be open to any messages that are revealed.

Good.

Now, pick up your orange stone. This stone represents your sacral chakra. It is the source for creativity and emotion as well as fertility and reproduction of life or ideas. Our ability to manifest desires occurs from this chakra. Sensuality, intimacy, and connection are enhanced when this chakra is clear. Take on the energy of this stone and focus on its uniqueness. Place the stone slightly below your belly button and hold it in place until its orange light is strong, clear, and pure, projecting towards the ocean in front of you. How does your orange light appear? If it is not bright and fully projected, ask Spirit to help clear and heal this area. Concentrate and pull from the energy of your orange stone until you feel the light is as it should be. Once your orange light is strong and pure, place it between your legs. Continue being open to receiving messages that are revealed.

Good.

Next, you may pick up your yellow stone. This stone represents your solar plexus chakra. This is your center for instinct, intellect, and awareness of self. When this chakra is clear your sense of personal power, confidence, and responsibility are more reliable. Self-esteem, willpower, self-discipline, and personality radiates from this chakra. From this center you will always feel what is right. This is your core center that provides clear understanding but only if it is functioning at full capacity. Again, take on the energy of this stone and focus on its uniqueness. Place the stone in the center of your stomach slightly above or level with your belly button. Hold it there until its yellow light is strong, clear, and pure, projecting towards the ocean in front of you. Notice the quality of your yellow light. If it is not bright and fully projected, ask Spirit to help clear and heal this area for you. Concentrate and pull from the energy of your yellow stone until you feel the light is as it should be. Once your yellow light is strong and pure, place it between your legs. Remember to listen for messages that may be revealed.

Okay.

Now, pick up your green and pink stones. These stones represent your heart chakra. From here you find healing and share the ability to love and be loved. It is the center for self-respect, self-love, and connectedness with others. This chakra represents emotional balance and can bring you overall harmony, peace, and the ability to show compassion when not tainted. Like before take on the energy of this stone and focus on its uniqueness. Now hold the stone over your heart until its pink and green light is strong, clear, and pure, projecting towards the ocean in front of you. Again, notice how your colors appear. If they are not bright and fully projected, ask Spirit to help clear and heal this area. Concentrate and pull from the energy of your pink and green stones until you feel the light is as it should be. Once your lights are strong and pure, place the stones between your legs. Do you see, hear, or feel any messages being revealed?

Great.

Now you may pick up your blue stone. This represents your throat chakra. This center holds your ability to communicate. It is the first of the three higher spiritual chakras. It represents your inner voice. When cleared this is your center for sharing and seeking truths. Creativity and authenticity also stem from this chakra. Take on the energy of this stone and focus on its uniqueness. Hold the stone against your throat until its blue light is strong, clear, and pure, projecting towards the ocean in front of you. How does your light appear? If it is not bright and fully projected, ask Spirit to help clear and heal this area. Concentrate and pull from the energy of your blue stone until you feel the light is as it should be. Once your blue light is strong and pure, place it between your legs. Can you sense any messages being revealed?

Okay.

Next, pick up your indigo stone. This stone represents your third eye/brow chakra. It is the center for opening higher planes of the spirit world and elevating consciousness. It helps with clear thinking, gifts of spiritual contemplation, and self-reflection. This chakra allows us to access deeper truths and to see beyond the mind or words. Now, as before, take on the energy of this stone and focus on its uniqueness. Gently press the stone in the center of your eyebrows and hold it in place until its light is strong, clear, and pure, projecting towards the ocean in front of you. Notice how your light appears. If it is not bright and fully projected, ask Spirit to help clear and heal this area. Concentrate and pull from the energy of your stone until you feel the light is as it should be. Once your light is strong and pure, place it between your legs. Don't forget to pay attention to any messages being revealed.

Good.

Finally, pick up your purple/white stone. This stone represents your crown chakra. It is the top of the chakra "ladder." Just as the base chakra grounds us to Earth energy by being at the bottom of the "ladder," the crown chakra connects us with the Divine Source of creation from a level of higher awareness of the universe and connectedness to Spirit or spirituality. When this chakra is clear you have a more vivid awareness of a deeper meaning to life and our oneness with others and nature. Absorb the energy of this stone and focus on its uniqueness. Rest the stone on top of your head/crown until its light is strong, clear, and pure, projecting towards the ocean in front of you. Just as before notice how this light appears. If it is not bright and fully projected, ask Spirit to help clear and heal this area for you. Concentrate and pull from the energy of your stone until you feel the light is as it should be. Once your white light is strong and pure, place it between your legs. Remain open to receiving any messages that are revealed.

Great.

Now, look out toward the ocean and notice all your vibrant colors swirling in front of you. They are very powerful, pure, and clear. As you focus on the colors show gratitude towards Spirit for clearing areas that needed healing and for raising your energy to a higher place today. Now, slowly breathe in and watch as your colors begin to mix together, gradually starting to retreat from the ocean back into your heart center. Embrace the energy as it enters into your heart and travels up and down your spine, bouncing back and forth from your root chakra to your crown chakra. Take a moment to bask in this beautiful energy.

Okay.

Now this time, as your swirling colorful light heads towards your crown chakra, prepare to let it exit from the top of your head. Ready. Go. Now push the light from the top of your head out into the universe to help and heal others.

Great.

Once again, notice your surroundings. Feel the sand underneath you and savor one more crisp ocean breeze against your face. Then pick up your stones, place them back into your basket, and prepare to return to your present place.

*Inhale, hold, one . . . two . . . three . . . now exhale.
Begin slowly to come back to the present place
and time.*

*Again, inhale, hold, one . . . two . . . three . . . now
exhale. Now become aware of your body, how it
is positioned, and start to move your arms, legs,
hands, and feet.*

*Once more, inhale, hold, one . . . two . . . three . . .
now exhale. When you are ready, slowly open
your eyes and return to your original state.*

JOURNAL SPACE

What colors or scents were present?

_____

_____

What sensations did you feel?

_____

_____

What messages did you see or hear?

_____

_____

Were you familiar with the place or any objects or people that were present?

_____

_____

What questions can you remember and answer from this meditation?

_____

_____

What caught your attention most during this journey?

_____

_____

What information would you most like to remember about this experience?

_____

_____

How can you apply information received from this experience to your current place in life?

_____

_____

What did you learn about yourself on this journey?

_____

_____

If there is one thing you could improve about your soul journey, starting today, what would that be?

_____

_____

What else would you like to remember about this experience?

_____

_____

Are there any unanswered questions or ideas sparked from this meditation that you would like to learn more about?

_____

_____

Continue writing about anything else special to you from this meditation.

_____

_____

CREATIVE ARTWORK SPACE

Under the Veil Energy Raising Meditation

Close your eyes and find a comfortable position. You may sit up with your feet flat on the floor or lie down. Whichever you prefer is great.

We are going to start by taking three deep breaths. Okay, let's begin.

Here we go, first breath. Inhale, hold, one . . . two . . . three . . . now exhale. Notice your face and shoulders start to relax.

Okay, again, inhale, hold, one . . . two . . . three . . . now exhale. Notice your legs and arms start to relax, and then your entire body.

One more time, inhale, hold, one . . . two . . . three . . . now exhale. The stresses of your day are melting away. You are now ready for the journey.

Now, imagine yourself standing in front of a dark curtain. The curtain can be whatever color you choose. The room around you is dark, and all you can see is the curtain directly in front of you. You are close enough to this curtain for your nose to brush against it. Notice if you smell or sense anything familiar about this curtain or place. Now, slowly bend down and grasp the bottom of the curtain. As you clench the curtain, notice the texture of it. Grasp it very firmly and feel the anticipation begin to build as you prepare to lift the curtain.

Good.

Now, start by slowly raising the curtain up to your knees, then up to your waist, and now to your chest. Notice the warmth and light coming from behind the curtain as you raise it higher and higher. The light from the other side is getting brighter and brighter as you raise the curtain above your head. Suddenly you duck underneath and are immediately blinded by the gleam of sunlight beaming directly in front of you. As you step fully under the curtain, you can now drop it and watch as the curtain disappears.

Great.

Now, notice you are standing on the ledge of a very rocky cliff overlooking a brilliant ocean. The sun is still directly ahead but your eyes are now adjusting. The sun is warm, welcoming, and no longer blinding. Now, look down at your feet and notice how they are positioned. Notice that you are safe despite being on the edge of a cliff. Take a deep breath, and quietly thank Spirit for bringing you on this journey.

Good.

Now, slowly begin to look up and focus straight ahead. You know that your feet are firmly planted. You know that the ocean is below you. You can hear the waves crashing and feel the saltwater mist against your face. You can smell the ocean water that gives life to so much. You are one with your surroundings, and therefore you feel safe to look straight ahead. As you begin to focus your eyes forward, notice the shadows of other beings standing off to the right and left of your path toward the sun. Try to recognize the shadows. Some may be in the shape of a person or being. Others may be in the shape of an animal. Notice and remember what figures come to life for you. How are they standing? What are they wearing? Are they looking at you? Are they waving for you to come closer? Can you hear any of them speak? If so what are they saying? Stand still and soak in all that you notice, feel, hear, or think.

Good.

Now, I would like you to ask one of the beings you noticed to step out of the crowd. Make note of how this specific person or being looks and feels to you. Ask this person or being to reveal themselves to you. Note any words, images, or feelings you get as you hear the answer to your question.

Good.

Next, notice the actions of your chosen person or being. Notice how they motion for you to come forward into the sun to join them. As your person or being motions for you, notice how all the other shadows in line become clearer as well. Notice how they are all cheering for you. With spiritual chants and joyful dance, they encourage you to draw nearer to them. They begin to join hands, and as they do so, you can feel the energy they project begin to pull you off the ledge. Take a deep breath, relax, trust, and just allow the energy to pull you closer and closer to the edge. Feel your toes leave the rocky ledge, then the soles of your feet. Now, as your heels approach the edge, relax one last time, allowing the energy of all these incredible beings to sweep you off the cliff and carry you towards the sun.

Good.

Wow, you are flying. Stretch your arms out in front of you and start projecting a strong, pure, bright white beam of light from your fingertips. Extend the light like a rope shooting out towards your group of beings. Notice the light from your fingers feels warm and powerful. Focus on these light beams and try to make them brighter, longer, and stronger. Keep going. Stretch your light beams further and further out until the rope of light moves closer to your group of helpers. Now, one last time, take a deep breath and push your light ropes out, one last big push, and POW! Your light rope is now one with the light of your helpers. You are fully connected and the energy between your helpers and yourself continues to grow increasingly stronger. It feels as if you are flying much faster than before. As your speed accelerates, you look up and realize you are nearing the sun. The sun that once seemed unreachable from the rocky cliff is now at the tip of your fingertips. As you grower closer to the sun, you feel the warmth intensify. The brightness becomes overwhelming and the vibration of energy in your hands is now felt within your whole body. You are forced to close your eyes. Just embrace this flying experience as the excitement builds and energy magnifies. Know that this journey is coming to an end so take in every detail of the experience. How do you feel? What do you see differently with your eyes shut? Can you hear anything? One last time take a deep breath and notice how incredible this energy feels. Remember how intense your light beam cord was when connected to your helpers. Take the experience in and recognize you are a powerful vessel of energy. Tell yourself that you can always project this energy. Know that you can use this energy to lift your spirit when you are down, to recharge you when you feel depleted, and to empower you to achieve all that you are meant to be. Understand this energy lives in you and is you, and therefore you control it.

Good.

Now, slowly pull your hands back to your body. Look at your fingers and realize the light beam rope is now disappearing and fading into your hands. You are no longer connected to your helpers. They are becoming only shadows of the figures you first saw. As they disappear, show gratitude for their help. Look towards the sun that is so close and thank it for the warmth and direction it provided. Now, turn around and look down.

Good.

Notice you are back on the rocky cliff. The ocean is again beneath you and your feet feel very solid. Blink! Blink! And once more blink! Now you are behind the curtain. Take a deep breath, exhale, and smile. It is time to come back from your wonderful energized journey.

Inhale, hold, one . . . two . . . three . . . now exhale.
Begin slowly to come back to the present place
and time.

Again, inhale, hold, one . . . two . . . three . . . now
exhale. Now become aware of your body, how it
is positioned, and start to move your arms, legs,
hands, and feet.

Once more, inhale, hold, one . . . two . . . three . . .
now exhale. When you are ready, slowly open your
eyes and return to your original state.

JOURNAL SPACE

What colors or scents were present?

_____

_____

_____

What sensations did you feel?

_____

_____

_____

What messages did you see or hear?

_____

_____

_____

Were you familiar with the place or any objects or people that were present?

_____

_____

_____

What questions can you remember and answer from this meditation?

_____

_____

_____

What caught your attention most during this journey?

_____

_____

_____

What information would you most like to remember about this experience?

_____

_____

_____

How can you apply information received from this experience to your current place in life?

_____

_____

What did you learn about yourself on this journey?

_____

_____

If there is one thing you could improve about your soul journey, starting today, what would that be?

_____

_____

What else would you like to remember about this experience?

_____

_____

Are there any unanswered questions or ideas sparked from this meditation that you would like to learn more about?

_____

_____

Continue writing about anything else special to you from this meditation.

_____

_____

CREATIVE ARTWORK SPACE

Disconnecting from Negative Energy Attachments Meditation

Close your eyes and find a comfortable position.
You may sit up with your feet flat on the floor or
lie down. Whichever you prefer is great.

We are going to start by taking three deep
breaths. Okay, Here we go, first breath. Inhale,
hold, one . . . two . . . three . . . now exhale. Notice
your face and shoulders start to relax.

Okay, again, inhale, hold, one . . . two . . . three
. . . now exhale. Notice your legs and arms start
to relax, and then your entire body.

One more time, inhale, hold, one . . . two . . . three
. . . now exhale. The stresses of your day are melting away. You are now ready for the journey.

Imagine you are standing in a warehouse. Notice the floors and walls are made of concrete. Your surroundings are cold, stale, and uninviting. You begin to wonder why you are here. What has brought you to an environment so unwelcoming? For reasons unknown to you in this moment, you are unable to move. As you remain frozen, you can smell the dampness around you. The warehouse is empty and void. The lighting is dim forcing you to adjust your eyes. As your vision balances, you notice an aisle full of metal boxes leading to a dead-end wall. Take a moment and absorb all the details of your surroundings. Become familiar with this place, as uncomfortable as it may be. Remember all you can about what you see, feel, hear, or sense. Remember all that is presented to you, so you will not forget where you started today.

Good.

Now, attempt to move your feet. Notice you can wiggle and stretch your legs again. Once you feel sturdy enough to walk, head in the direction of the aisle. Keep walking until you reach the aisle of boxes. As you enter the aisle, notice that all the boxes are labeled and have power outlets on the outside. Begin to read the labels and make note of them in your mind. Some of the boxes read:

"I can't," "I won't," "You can't," "You won't," "You'll never," "You are worthless," "No one cares," "You aren't smart enough," "You aren't attractive enough," and/or "You don't deserve better."

Some of the boxes exhibit names of people who are familiar to you, such as *those who were part of past hurtful relationships or friendships. Some boxes even display names of family members or children.*

Some of the boxes are blank and only reveal a message as you pass by them. Please trust that theses secret messages are for your eyes only. *These messages may be symbolic of painful or traumatic experiences or reminders of scarring confrontations.*

As you read the many boxes, I'd like you to recognize which ones you feel most connected with.. Notice how some of the boxes grasp your attention more than others. Pay attention to how you feel when reading some of the familiar words or messages. Recall which of the boxes leave you feeling very negative or weighed down. Are there boxes that make you feel scared or angry? Do some of the messages leave you feeling very sad or broken? Take a moment and identify which boxes feel as though they are a part of who you are in this present moment of your journey.

Good.

Now, continue to walk towards the dead-end wall. Notice how heavy you are feeling. It is getting harder and harder to walk as you near the exit of the aisle. As you approach the end of the aisle, you start to feel pulled backwards, but you know you can't and shouldn't go back. In an attempt to identify what is pulling at your legs you look down to find there are multiple electric cords exiting your body. You turn around to make sense of what is happening. You notice the cords connected to you are also plugged into all the boxes on the shelves that you felt a connection with. The boxes are glowing bright red as if warning you of the danger to your soul. The brighter the boxes glow, the harder the cords tug at you, attempting to pull you back into the aisle. These damaging connections are draining you of energy, of your very life/soul force. Desperate to leave the aisle, you look towards the wall for escape and notice it is now glowing bright white. You realize if you can get to the wall you will be safe and replenished. With every ounce of energy that remains, you start running towards the wall. Your legs are heavy but you press harder and harder. Your legs burn from the strength it is taking to move ahead, and right as you feel you can't go any further, your hands touch the glowing wall. Ahhhh! Finally, you are safe, but you know you are not yet finished. You turn towards the aisle of boxes and with great fierceness begin yanking out the cords that are exiting your body. As you destroy each connection, you notice the box it was attached to goes black and your body feels lighter and brighter just like the wall you are resting against. For each attachment you demolish you speak to the message it represents, validating that it no longer has any power over you. You are feeling empowered, no longer depleted. Now continue to rip each cord from your body until there are no more connections. Rip, rip, rip, and pull harder. Keep going. Now throw all the connections to the side of you. Look at the pile of cords completely powerless and useless. Remember you destroyed all ties connecting you to the negative energies that tried attacking you. You are once again in control of your soul life force. You are reenergized and purified of all past connection to the aisle of depletion and doubt.

Good.

Now, take a deep breath and rest against the glowing bright white wall. Notice how much better you feel. Despite the energy exerted to remove the cords, you find that you are at peace. You begin to see, feel, and hear things around you. Notice any scents or familiarity of this place. Just take a moment and commune with the positive vibration the wall is sending you. Absorb the healing, rejuvenating, bright, white light. Compare the heaviness you first felt in the warehouse to the way you feel resting against the wall. As you relax every muscle in your body, close your eyes and feel your body begin to melt into the light of the wall. As you do this, prepare to return from your journey.

Inhale, hold, one ... two ... three ... now exhale. Begin slowly to come back to the present place and time.

Again, inhale, hold, one ... two ... three ... now exhale. Now become aware of your body, how it is positioned, and start to move your arms, legs, hands, and feet.

Once more, inhale, hold, one ... two ... three ... now exhale. When you are ready, slowly open your eyes and return to your original state.

JOURNAL SPACE

What colors or scents were present?

_____

_____

_____

What sensations did you feel?

_____

_____

_____

What messages did you see or hear?

_____

_____

_____

Were you familiar with the place or any objects or people that were present?

_____

_____

_____

What questions can you remember and answer from this meditation?

_____

_____

_____

What caught your attention most during this journey?

_____

_____

_____

What information would you most like to remember about this experience?

_____

_____

_____

How can you apply information received from this experience to your current place in life?

_____

_____

What did you learn about yourself on this journey?

_____

_____

If there is one thing you could improve about your soul journey, starting today, what would that be?

_____

_____

What else would you like to remember about this experience?

_____

_____

Are there any unanswered questions or ideas sparked from this meditation that you would like to learn more about?

_____

_____

Continue writing about anything else special to you from this meditation.

_____

_____

CREATIVE ARTWORK SPACE

Declutter Your Energy Space Meditation

Close your eyes and find a comfortable position. You may sit up with your feet flat on the floor or lie down. Whichever you prefer is great.

We are going to start by taking three deep breaths. Okay, Here we go, first breath. Inhale, hold, one . . . two . . . three . . . now exhale. Notice your face and shoulders start to relax.

Okay, again, inhale, hold, one . . . two . . . three . . . now exhale. Notice your legs and arms start to relax, and then your entire body.

One more time, inhale, hold, one . . . two . . . three . . . now exhale. The stresses of your day are melting away. You are now ready for the journey.

Imagine you are sitting at a desk. The desk is in disarray. Nothing is organized and you are frustrated with the idea of having to clean the pile of clutter before you. You consider throwing everything away and simply starting over. Just as you are about to sweep off the desk, pushing all the junk into the trash, you notice a small shiny black stone hidden in the center of all this mess. You dig through the crumbled papers and clear the area around the stone. The stone's energy holds such a solid presence that you know not to move it. Instead you take a moment and admire its beauty. You are surprised that such a colorless stone can be so attractive to you. As you focus harder on the stone, you notice it is calling out to you. Pause for a moment and listen. Do you hear anything? Do you see or feel messages the stone is sending? Pause and listen to what you are getting.

Good.

Now, continue to stare into this black stone, but this time be aware of how it is changing. The stone is growing larger. As the stone is growing larger the junk and mess is slowly disappearing too. It's as if the stone is absorbing the clutter from your desk. With every piece of paper or object it absorbs the stone grows larger in size. As you watch, it suddenly occurs to you that the mess on your desk represents negative, overwhelming, thoughts, ideas, people, or situations that are bothersome and often consuming. Project these negative energies at the stone for it to absorb just as it continues to absorb and clear objects from the desk. Send all this heavy, ugly energy that does not serve your higher good to the stone and release it to be destroyed forever.

Good.

When you are finished and the desk is clear notice the magnitude of the stone before you. Take in every detail of the stone and quietly thank Spirit for relieving you of the heaviness of negative energy symbolized by the new size of a once small black stone.

Good.

Now, prepare to destroy the black, heavy, engulfed stone. You can destroy it however you choose. Be creative. You may want to blow it up or chisel it away until only dust remains. You may choose to shrink it for future use. Or you may want to feel the satisfaction of pushing it out the window in front of you, so it is removed from your presence completely. Either way take this time to destroy your stone.

Great.

Now that your stone is destroyed, pause a moment and enjoy the serenity of your newly cleared desk. Sit and absorb the pure, positive energy around you. Feel the lightness in the room around you. Take a deep breath and inhale the scent of a newly cleared, clean atmosphere. Look towards the window once more, close your eyes, and inhale deeply in preparation for your return.

Inhale, hold, one . . . two . . . three . . . now exhale. Begin slowly to come back to the present place and time.

Again, inhale, hold, one . . . two . . . three . . . now exhale. Now become aware of your body, how it is positioned, and start to move your arms, legs, hands, and feet.

Once more, inhale, hold, one . . . two . . . three . . . now exhale. When you are ready, slowly open your eyes and return to your original state.

JOURNAL SPACE

What colors or scents were present?

_____

_____

What sensations did you feel?

_____

_____

What messages did you see or hear?

_____

_____

_____

Were you familiar with the place or any objects or people that were present?

_____

_____

What questions can you remember and answer from this meditation?

_____

_____

_____

What caught your attention most during this journey?

_____

_____

What information would you most like to remember about this experience?

_____

_____

How can you apply information received from this experience to your current place in life?

_____

_____

What did you learn about yourself on this journey?

_____

_____

If there is one thing you could improve about your soul journey, starting today, what would that be?

_____

_____

What else would you like to remember about this experience?

_____

_____

Are there any unanswered questions or ideas sparked from this meditation that you would like to learn more about?

_____

_____

Continue writing about anything else special to you from this meditation.

_____

_____

CREATIVE ARTWORK SPACE

Daily Cleansing
of Negativity
Meditation

Close your eyes and find a comfortable position.
You may sit up with your feet flat on the floor or
lie down. Whichever you prefer is great.

We are going to start by taking three deep breaths.
Okay, Here we go, first breath. Inhale, hold, one
. . . two . . . three . . . now exhale. Notice your
face and shoulders start to relax.

Okay, again, inhale, hold, one . . . two . . . three
. . . now exhale. Notice your legs and arms start to
relax, and then your entire body.

One more time, inhale, hold, one . . . two . . . three
. . . now exhale. The stresses of your day are
melting away. You are now ready for the journey.

Imagine you are sitting on a train. As you look around, notice you are alone. The gorgeous scenery outside your window catches your attention. You feel calm and safe. Your eyes begin to close as you rest from the serenity of this place. Out of nowhere, people begin to run aboard the train. With each body that boards you start to feel anxious and weighed down. The peaceful state you obtained when alone on the train is quickly dissolving as you lose control of your personal energy and space. Each person that boards appears to drain more and more life from you. Just as you start to feel like you can't breathe the doors of the train close and it begins to take off. Okay, good, now you can catch your breath. The movement of the train gives you hope that no other negative energies will board for now. But wait, if movement ensures no other passengers can board, does it also mean you are left with no escape from the current passengers? As you ponder this question the passengers begin to look familiar to you. You see coworkers, bosses, friends, relatives, partners, and spouses. You see faces of some who you do not know but ran across throughout your day. You realize right away the meaning of this journey. The people who boarded the train are souls you connect with in your daily life whether by choice or chance. During contact with these individuals, you allow them to jump aboard and deplete your personal energy and space, which is symbolized by how they boarded the train without permission. The peacefulness you felt when alone on the train represented you being in control of your energy, cleared, grounded, and positive at the start of each day. But as the passengers boarded you noticed how easily they depleted you of your life source by intruding on your personal space. Take a moment and reflect on the effects the passengers had on you. How does this translate into your daily life? Who are the passengers on your train? Do you notice any connections? Absorb any messages being shared with you in this moment.

Good.

Now that you understand your role on the train, take a moment to identify the specific individuals you see around you. Make note of those who deplete your energy in order to avoid relations with them in the future. Recognize changes you can make to stop these passengers from boarding your train uninvited. Now look at the screen above you and notice the train is stopping soon. Yay!!! With the upcoming stop you can finally dismiss these passengers. Anticipation heightens as you gain control again. From now on, you will decide who boards and if they may stay. As the train approaches its stop, you confront each individual, blessing and thanking them for the lesson they have taught you. Once you have spoken to all the passengers, the train comes to an abrupt stop and the doors open. You watch as each passenger exits the train. With each good-bye, excitement and joys enters your heart making you feel lighter and more at ease again. Off they go, again and again. You feel your personal power return and truly believe you are in control. Take a moment to embrace these wonderful new enlightenments and clear out the entire train.

Great.

As the last person exits, take a deep breath, and as you exhale, imagine you are blowing away any residual negativity on your train. Cleanse your train. Cleanse this personal space of power and peace. Then find your original seat. Notice the scenery once more as you start to gaze out the window. Absorb the

positivity around you. Close your eyes and take in the serenity around you. Thank Spirit for giving you awareness of the
control you possess over who may board your train. As you
embrace the vibration of energy from the space around you,
inhale and prepare to return from this journey.

Inhale, hold, one . . . two . . . three . . . now exhale. Begin slowly to come back to the present place and time.

Again, inhale, hold, one . . . two . . . three . . . now exhale. Now become aware of your body, how it is positioned, and start to move your arms, legs, hands, and feet.

Once more, inhale, hold, one . . . two . . . three . . . now exhale. When you are ready, slowly open your eyes and return to your original state.

JOURNAL SPACE

What colors or scents were present?

_____

_____

What sensations did you feel?

_____

_____

What messages did you see or hear?

_____

_____

Were you familiar with the place or any objects or people that were present?

_____

_____

What questions can you remember and answer from this meditation?

_____

_____

What caught your attention most during this journey?

_____

_____

What information would you most like to remember about this experience?

_____

_____

How can you apply information received from this experience to your current place in life?

_____

_____

What did you learn about yourself on this journey?

_____

_____

If there is one thing you could improve about your soul journey, starting today, what would that be?

_____

_____

What else would you like to remember about this experience?

_____

_____

Are there any unanswered questions or ideas sparked from this meditation that you would like to learn more about?

_____

_____

Continue writing about anything else special to you from this meditation.

_____

_____

CREATIVE ARTWORK SPACE

Enhanced Higher Consciousness Dreaming Meditation

Close your eyes and find a comfortable position. You may sit up with your feet flat on the floor or lie down. Whichever you prefer is great.

We are going to start by taking three deep breaths. Okay, let's begin.

Here we go, first breath. Inhale, hold, one . . . two . . . three . . . now exhale. Notice your face and shoulders start to relax.

Okay, again, inhale, hold, one . . . two . . . three . . . now exhale. Notice your legs and arms start to relax, and then your entire body.

One more time, inhale, hold, one . . . two . . . three . . . now exhale. The stresses of your day are melting away. You are now ready for the journey.

Imagine you are at the base of a huge mountain. The terrain ahead is a mix of forestry and rocky cliffs. You realize you are alone. The only other life around is that of Mother Nature, and you are in need of preparation before starting the journey up this mountain. You grab the backpack you have been carrying and open it to recheck all the items you brought for the journey. One by one you pull out items and evaluate their purpose, checking them off your list and placing them as needed back into your bag. First, you pull out a water bottle and food to help sustain life and energy while ascending. Next, you pull out an extendable hiking stick to help with terrain that is more treacherous. Then you reach deep down into your bag and begin pulling out beautifully colored, very unique stones. One stone is black to help absorb and prevent any negative energy from affecting you. There are pink and green stones to aid in healing on the journey. There are purple and white stones to keep your intuition heightened and your mind focused on the higher purpose for coming. Next, you pull out a deep red stone. This stone is special and will solidly ground you so that you do not ascend past any level that is not for your higher good up this mountain and beyond. Its grounding abilities will help you to more easily come back down whenever the time is right. As you pull the last item from your bag you realize your journey is almost ready to begin. You slowly unzip the front pocket and pull out a shiny white ball. As you touch this ball to the top of your head, you are immediately covered in a flowing white light of protection. Now you are ready to begin. You are grounded, protected, and prepared for the journey up the mountain into higher realms of the unconsciousness. Gather your things and start walking.

Good.

Keep walking. Now, begin pulling yourself up and around the rocky terrain. Keep going, push harder and harder until you near the top of the mountain. Use your stick to gain footing on the slippery ledges and grab the surrounding tree limbs as leverage to hurl your body up higher and higher, closer and closer to the top. Keep going. You are almost there. Now you have come to a flat landing of rock and trees. Take a moment, stop, and consume some of your water and food. Look down at how far you have come. Notice your shield of white light is still glowing bright and completely covering you. Nothing can harm you. Your red stone is grounding you. Your feet feel solid on the earth around you. Your pink and green stones have healed all the past you left behind with each step higher and closer to the top. The purple and white stones are encouraging you to go higher. The black stone is continuing to absorb any negative energy that would prevent you from going higher or acknowledging all you have achieved so far. Now, as you finish your food and water, look ahead, and with every ounce of determination to fulfill your purpose in this journey, begin ascending again. This time do not stop until you reach the top.

Good.

Now, you have reached the top of the mountain. But your journey is not over. The ascent up the mountain was proof you could do the hard work and preparation for the journey, but now is your time to fly. As you gaze out into the valley below you, suddenly eagles, larger than you have ever seen begin flying around. As they are circling one speaks your name. You reach out your hand to grab the feathers and pull yourself up onto this magnificent creature's back. Now you are flying with the incredible life force of the air. You are still covered in white light and finally feel not only protected but at peace. Now you can truly rest. You lay your head against the eagles back and fall asleep as the he flies you to and fro, over and under, higher and higher into realms of unconsciousness you have never seen before. As you sleep, absorbing all the energy around you, also listen for words or messages that are given. Remember details, pictures, or visions you may receive from this experience. Take all of this life force in and when you are ready, slowly rub your eyes and sit up while still holding onto the eagle as he begins to fly downward back toward the mountain. As the bird descends pull out your red stone, hold it tightly in your hand, and thank Spirit for this amazing creature and for allowing you on this journey. As you grip the red stone and request once again to be grounded, the eagle swoops to the bottom of the mountain and safely drops you off, then disappears into thin air. Now your feet are on solid ground. Take a moment and regain your balance. Acknowledge your surroundings once more. Look up at the mountain you defeated and remember the heights and depths of unconsciousness you experienced on this journey. As you turn to walk away, place your red stone back into your backpack, shrink your protective white light for future use, and close your eyes to prepare to return from this journey.

Inhale, hold, one . . . two . . . three . . . now exhale.
Begin slowly to come back to the present place
and time.

Again, inhale, hold, one . . . two . . . three . . . now
exhale. Now become aware of your body, how it
is positioned, and start to move your arms, legs,
hands, and feet.

Once more, inhale, hold, one . . . two . . . three . . .
now exhale. When you are ready, slowly open your
eyes and return to your original state.

JOURNAL SPACE

What colors or scents were present?

_____

_____

_____

What sensations did you feel?

_____

_____

_____

What messages did you see or hear?

_____

_____

_____

Were you familiar with the place or any objects or people that were present?

_____

_____

_____

What questions can you remember and answer from this meditation?

_____

_____

_____

What caught your attention most during this journey?

_____

_____

_____

What information would you most like to remember about this experience?

_____

_____

_____

How can you apply information received from this experience to your current place in life?

What did you learn about yourself on this journey?

If there is one thing you could improve about your soul journey, starting today, what would that be?

What else would you like to remember about this experience?

Are there any unanswered questions or ideas sparked from this meditation that you would like to learn more about?

Continue writing about anything else special to you from this meditation.

CREATIVE ARTWORK SPACE

Spirit Tree Grounding Meditation

Close your eyes and find a comfortable position. You may sit up with your feet flat on the floor or lie down. Whichever you prefer is great.

We are going to start by taking three deep breaths. Okay, let's begin.

Here we go, first breath. Inhale, hold, one . . . two . . . three . . . now exhale. Notice your face and shoulders start to relax.

Okay, again, inhale, hold, one . . . two . . . three . . . now exhale. Notice your legs and arms start to relax, and then your entire body.

One more time, inhale, hold, one . . . two . . . three . . . now exhale. The stresses of your day are melting away. You are now ready for the journey.

Now, imagine you are standing barefoot in an open field. The field is full of beautiful flowers and tall grass. Notice how vibrant the colors of the flowers are. Notice the grass is green and crisp. Look down at your feet and begin to squish them into the dirt. Feel the warm, damp dirt between your toes. Take another deep breath in and quietly whisper thank you to Mother Earth for allowing you to connect with her today.

Now, notice the fresh scent of the flowers and grass in the open field. Feel the wind as it begins to gently blow by you. What direction is the breeze blowing? Can you feel the warmth of the sun radiating on your back? Notice how relaxed and happy you are. Notice that your mind is calm and peaceful, only focused on what you feel and see in this moment. As you embrace this moment, you suddenly realize you have been here before. The familiarity of this place creates a calmness within. You now trust and know that it is okay and safe to begin this journey.

Good.

Now, slowly begin to walk forward. What other things do you notice? Are there ladybugs or butterflies landing on the flowers? Can you hear or see any animals hiding in the tall grass. Are there birds chirping and flying overhead?

Good.

Now, slowly start to look up from the noticing the ground around you. As your eyes focus forward, you see the edge of a forest. Begin to walk faster towards the forest. Walk faster and faster until you are jogging toward the forest. Notice the texture of the grass and flowers as you pass through them. Feel the wind pick up as your pace quickens. You are now approaching the edge of the forest. Your heart beats a little quicker and the colors you were seeing start to fade into more vivid shades of green. You stop suddenly! You have reached the forest.

The forest is different than the field. The dirt is cooler to the touch. You gain your footing and begin to walk deeper into the forest. The sun is no longer bright, as you are protected by the shade of all the magnificent, giant trees towering over you. You notice every tree looks slightly different. Some trees are smooth and others have rough sharp edges. Some of the trees have huge, widened trunks that tell their age and wisdom while others are more newly developed and show signs of youth. Some of the trees have billowing limbs weighed down by leaves while others seems much more airy and light. Look more closely at the trees and notice if any of them are bearing fruit, nuts, or blossoms. Do you notice any other distinctive features of the trees?

Okay, good.

Now, turn around in a circle noticing all the trees around you, then pick your favorite tree. Remember, glance at all of them first. Of the trees you have noticed while in the forest, pick the tree of your choice, the tree that speaks most to you, the tree that feels like it is yours and can protect you, provide shelter for you, and give you a sense of connection to Mother Earth then go up to it.

Good.

Once you have reached your tree, connect with it and embrace it in whatever manner you choose. Touch the bark and connect with your trees texture, hug it to combine life energies, or even just sit at its base, whatever you choose.

Good.

Now we are going to imagine ourselves one with our tree. Think about what is special about your tree. What made you choose this tree? Remember these things. Do you share similarities with your tree? Can you find a connection that you both share? Does any image, word, or idea of your connectedness come to mind as you are communing with your tree?

Good.

Now, focus on what nourishes your tree. What allows your tree to thrive? Think about the roots that are growing beneath you giving life to this amazing piece of nature. Imagine how wide spread the roots are. Imagine how interconnected the roots of your tree are to the trees around it. Imagine the roots going deeper, deeper down into the earth soaking up clear, pure water along the way.

Good.

Now, stand up by your tree and begin to squish your feet into the cool damp dirt around you. And as you take in a cleansing breath, imagine your feet beginning to sink into the earth. Relax your body, do not fight it, and just go with the gravity of this moment. As the earth continues to pull you down, imagine your feet are stretching deep, deep, and deeper down into Mother Earth like the roots of your tree. You are getting stronger the further down you are pulled. You are feeling nurtured as your feet absorb all the energy of the earth around you. You can feel the vibration of Mother Earth as you are being grounded in her strength. Your feet are now solid like the roots of your tree. You are stable, safe, and sturdy. Nothing can move you. You are strong and in control. Stand in this strength, allowing it to consume you. Take in a deep cleansing breath, and be thankful for this strength as it is now part of your soul and will be with you always.

Good.

Now it is time to come back. Begin slowly wiggling and loosening your feet and legs from the place you are planted. Pull your feet up from the earth, keep pulling up and up until you are out. Once you are free, turn to your tree and quietly express your gratitude. Once more, memorize the appearance of your tree, any smells that will remind you of it or any other characteristics that are special to your tree. Name your tree if you would like. Remember naming your tree will give life to it, and therefore you can easily call upon it whenever you choose.

Good.

Now, turn away from your tree and begin walking towards the edge of the forest. Walk faster, faster, faster, again until you are jogging towards the open field.

Stop. Catch your breath.

You are back in the open field, the sun is shining on you, and the warmth of the ground between your toes is familiar and comforting. Once more, notice the beautiful flowers and reach out to touch the tall grass. As you feel the breeze begin to blow, take three deep breaths in.

Inhale, hold, one . . . two . . . three . . . now exhale. Begin slowly to come back to the present place and time.

Again, inhale, hold, one . . . two . . . three . . . now exhale. Now become aware of your body, how it is positioned, and start to move your arms, legs, hands, and feet.

Once more, inhale, hold, one . . . two . . . three . . . now exhale. When you are ready, slowly open your eyes and return to your original state.

JOURNAL SPACE

What colors or scents were present?

_____

_____

What sensations did you feel?

_____

_____

What messages did you see or hear?

_____

_____

Were you familiar with the place or any objects or people that were present?

_____

_____

What questions can you remember and answer from this meditation?

_____

_____

What caught your attention most during this journey?

_____

_____

What information would you most like to remember about this experience?

_____

_____

How can you apply information received from this experience to your current place in life?

_____

_____

What did you learn about yourself on this journey?

_____

_____

If there is one thing you could improve about your soul journey, starting today, what would that be?

_____

_____

What else would you like to remember about this experience?

_____

_____

Are there any unanswered questions or ideas sparked from this meditation that you would like to learn more about?

_____

_____

Continue writing about anything else special to you from this meditation.

_____

_____

CREATIVE ARTWORK SPACE

Spirit Flower Rebirthing Meditation

Close your eyes and find a comfortable position. You may sit up with your feet flat on the floor or lie down. Whichever you prefer is great.

We are going to start by taking three deep breaths. Okay, let's begin.

Here we go, first breath. Inhale, hold, one . . . two . . . three . . . now exhale. Notice your face and shoulders start to relax.

Okay, again, inhale, hold, one . . . two . . . three . . . now exhale. Notice your legs and arms start to relax, and then your entire body.

One more time, inhale, hold, one . . . two . . . three . . . now exhale. The stresses of your day are melting away. You are now ready for the journey.

Picture yourself sitting in a wooden canoe centered on a serene crystal clear pond. The water is aquamarine and gently flowing back and forth, back and forth, against the banks of the pond. Reach out and feel the crisp pureness of the water around you. Breathe in the refreshing summer's night air and relax with every breeze that swishes past your face as you row, row, row through the water. Take in all the scenery surrounding you. Pay attention to any details of the landscape that attract you. Embrace the experience and soak up the energy radiating from this enchanted place. As you row closer to the banks of this magnificent body of water, you feel excitement build. Anticipation of what lies ahead consumes you as you step out of your canoe onto solid ground. The earth underneath your feet feels cool and refreshing and is covered in green lush grass. You pull your canoe onto the bank and proceed to walk around. How do you feel standing on this peaceful ground? What emotions or thoughts come to you? Take a moment and familiarize yourself with this place.

Good.

Now, as you continue to walk around exploring the land, notice the changes occurring. With each step you take, a flower springs up from the earth in full bloom, showing its full potential and beauty. Each step in this new place is rebirthing a new part of your inner soul. The flowers are bursting out from the earth to reflect the act of you bursting out of your ego into who you are meant to be. As the flowers multiply, so do your ideas, dreams, aspirations, and inner strengths. Continue to walk until every detail of your life, every goal of improvement, and every manifested idea is fully bloomed, symbolically represented by the massive number of flowers multiplying around you. These flowers reflect your higher self and what you are meant to achieve in changing the world. Once you feel satisfied your field of flowers is complete, sit and rest amongst the beauty Spirit has shown you on this journey. Take a moment and notice every flower. Breathe in the scents all around. What colors do you see? What types of flowers are most present? Ask the flowers if there are any messages they would like to share. Ask the flowers to reveal their origin so that you may look up the deeper symbolism at a later time. Notice if your field is full of similar flowers or varied? Are you receiving any messages, words, or images? Slowly breathe and commune with your field of rebirth and aspirations.

Good.

Now, stand up with powerful intent on returning to your canoe and fulfilling your destined purpose. With fierce courage and positive light, walk towards the pond's edge. On the walk back, ask the flowers that will benefit you most in this part of your soul journey to show themselves. Ask those particular flowers to stick out higher than the rest in order for you to know they have chosen you. As the flowers present themselves, pick them and make a beautiful bouquet to take with you and cherish forever. Remember this experience as you look back once more before entering your canoe. Show gratitude to the flowers for showing up and sprouting as seeds of encouragement for you.

Good.

Now, climb into your canoe and begin to row back into the quiet, calm waters. Row, row, row. Keep going. As you near the center of the pond, hold the bouquet of flowers over your heart. Smile and breathe. Then prepare to return to your present state and place.

We are going to come back by taking three deep breaths. Inhale, hold, one . . . two . . . three . . . now exhale. Begin slowly to come back to the present place and time.

Again, inhale, hold, one . . . two . . . three . . . now exhale. Now become aware of your body, how it is positioned, and start to move your arms, legs, hands, and feet.

Once more, inhale, hold, one . . . two . . . three . . . now exhale. When you are ready, slowly open your eyes and return to your original state.

JOURNAL SPACE

What colors or scents were present?

_____

_____

What sensations did you feel?

_____

_____

What messages did you see or hear?

_____

_____

Were you familiar with the place or any objects or people that were present?

_____

_____

What questions can you remember and answer from this meditation?

_____

_____

What caught your attention most during this journey?

_____

_____

What information would you most like to remember about this experience?

_____

_____

How can you apply information received from this experience to your current place in life?

_____

_____

What did you learn about yourself on this journey?

_____

_____

If there is one thing you could improve about your soul journey, starting today, what would that be?

_____

_____

What else would you like to remember about this experience?

_____

_____

Are there any unanswered questions or ideas sparked from this meditation that you would like to learn more about?

_____

_____

Continue writing about anything else special to you from this meditation.

_____

_____

CREATIVE ARTWORK SPACE

Spirit Animal Gratitude Meditation

Close your eyes and find a comfortable position. You may sit up with your feet flat on the floor or lie down. Whichever you prefer is great.

We are going to start by taking three deep breaths. Okay, let's begin.

Here we go, first breath. Inhale, hold, one . . . two . . . three . . . now exhale. Notice your face and shoulders start to relax.

Okay, again, inhale, hold, one . . . two . . . three . . . now exhale. Notice your legs and arms start to relax, and then your entire body.

One more time, inhale, hold, one . . . two . . . three . . . now exhale. The stresses of your day are melting away. You are now ready for the journey.

Picture a beautiful dense forest of trees. You are standing in the forest looking ahead and you can see a glimmer of light trying to beam through the strong, sturdy, heavily leafed limbs of all the surrounding trees. Notice the texture of all the trees around you. Inhale deeply all the unique scents of the forest. With a big smile on your face, thank Mother Earth for her incredible creation.

Good.

Now, begin to walk toward the light you are seeing straight in front of you. Walk toward the light until you no longer are in the forest.

Good.

You have exited the forest. Look up and see the beautiful sunlight shining. Feel the warmth of her energy. Now look to your left, and you will see a huge boulder. Notched on the boulder is a large purple arrow pointing for you to stay straight on your path. Engraved under the arrow are the following words:

"Walk this way for your path is straight. Ahead lies the beginning of your evolution. Fear not as your destination is safe and will set you free."

Take in those words and begin to walk along the path in the direction of the arrow. As you begin to walk, you will notice a red wooden bridge up ahead. Hanging from the bridge is a ladder. The ladder is constructed with solid oak wood and painted bright white. You enter onto the bridge and notice the ladder has another purple arrow pointing down. You know you must follow the arrow. As you climb onto the ladder, notice the wood is strong and smooth. It is easy to grip and you realize how extremely safe you feel. In fact your excitement builds as you trust that this ladder is leading you down into a secret place that is only shared with those who believe in Spirit. At the bottom of the ladder you know you will get to meet spirit guides from the animal kingdom and that you will never be the same upon your return. As your anticipation builds, you begin to climb faster, down, down, down, until finally, THUD! Your feet hit solid ground.

Good.

Now your surroundings are darker, the sun is gone, but yet there is still a welcoming warmth to this place. There are hues of green all around, you can see and feel the rocky earth under your feet, and you can hear water flowing as if a river is nearby. Take in your surroundings, regain your balance, and start walking towards the sound of the water. While walking you begin to sense the presence of other life around you. The closer you get to the water the stronger the presence of these beings becomes. You can see shadows of creatures all around. They are guiding you to the water. Saturate yourself in the energy around you, and begin to listen for sounds, words, messages, or pictures being revealed. Do you notice specific colors? Can you smell distinct, familiar scents? Can you feel anything against your skin? As you near the water's edge, you notice the earth below you vibrating from all the energy of life this place offers. Stop at the water's edge and hold out your hand motioning for your spirit animals to reveal themselves. You may have one or two appear or you may attract an entire flock of animals, all eager to commune with you. Take note of all the animals you see. Show gratitude to them for coming. Tell the animals you look forward to calling upon them for help. Then ask for only those who are meant to help you presently in your life journey to stay. Tell the remaining animal guides that you now know where to find them and then give permission for them to leave and help others who need it.

Good.

Now, notice the animals that are left around you. Pay attention to how they are standing, if they are saying anything, and if they have any distinct features. Are they staying at a distance or are they eager to run to your side? Just be still and allow them to interact in the way they feel you most need them. Now, ask your spirit animals why they have chosen you and how they are meant to help on your journey. Ask them how you will know when they visit and what signs to look for when you need to know they are near and helping. Ask your spirit animals to reveal characteristics or strengths that you can gain from them. Finally, ask them to impart any last bit of knowledge or message they wish, as it is time for you to leave. Listen to your spirit animals as they reply, then take a moment and absorb their wonderful energy and love. Feel the warmth of these living spirit creatures. Show gratitude for their arrival in this journey, and tell them it is time for you to go.

Great.

Now turn around, look at your footprints on the ground and begin to follow them all the way back to the ladder. As you approach the ladder that helped you to descend into this enchanted place, look back one last time at all the magnificent creatures who came to meet you today. Wave good-bye and start to climb up the ladder. Climb higher, higher, and higher until now your hands can grasp the wooden rails of the red bridge. Pull yourself up onto the bridge and head in the direction of the boulder. Notice the boulder is now to your right, and the arrow is pointing in the direction of the forest. The sun is glowing bright again, and it is time to follow the arrow until you reach the edge of the forest. Notice the same smells and texture of the trees around you as you enter the forest. As soon as you recognize this familiar place, take in a deep breath, wait, and prepare to return back to the room you are sitting in.

Inhale, hold, one . . . two . . . three . . . now exhale. Begin slowly to come back to the present place and time.

Again, inhale, hold, one . . . two . . . three . . . now exhale. Now become aware of your body, how it is positioned, and start to move your arms, legs, hands, and feet.

Once more, inhale, hold, one . . . two . . . three . . . now exhale. When you are ready, slowly open your eyes and return to your original state.

JOURNAL SPACE

What colors or scents were present?

_____

_____

_____

What sensations did you feel?

_____

_____

_____

What messages did you see or hear?

_____

_____

_____

Were you familiar with the place or any objects or people that were present?

_____

_____

_____

What questions can you remember and answer from this meditation?

_____

_____

_____

What caught your attention most during this journey?

_____

_____

_____

What information would you most like to remember about this experience?

_____

_____

_____

How can you apply information received from this experience to your current place in life?

_____

_____

What did you learn about yourself on this journey?

_____

_____

If there is one thing you could improve about your soul journey, starting today, what would that be?

_____

_____

What else would you like to remember about this experience?

_____

_____

Are there any unanswered questions or ideas sparked from this meditation that you would like to learn more about?

_____

_____

Continue writing about anything else special to you from this meditation.

_____

CREATIVE ARTWORK SPACE

Spirit Guide Meditation

Close your eyes and find a comfortable position. You may sit up with your feet flat on the floor or lie down. Whichever you prefer is great.

We are going to start by taking three deep breaths. Okay, let's begin.

Here we go, first breath. Inhale, hold, one . . . two . . . three . . . now exhale. Notice your face and shoulders start to relax.

Okay, again, inhale, hold, one . . . two . . . three . . . now exhale. Notice your legs and arms start to relax, and then your entire body.

One more time, inhale, hold, one . . . two . . . three . . . now exhale. The stresses of your day are melting away. You are now ready for the journey.

Imagine yourself sitting around a huge inviting bonfire. It is a chilly fall evening. You can feel the crisp leaves all around. Acknowledge that you are comfortable and calm resting alongside this fire. Smell the scent of burning wood permeating your senses like that of a peace offering pipe. Listen to the crackling of the fire and feel the warmth radiating against your skin. The atmosphere is so serene that you feel your eyes begin to close. As your body attempts to drift into a deep restful state, suddenly you catch a glimpse of beings slowly moving from the shadows into the light of the bonfire. Your eyes pop open as you become very still, awaiting those who are nearing to reveal themselves. Now, take a minute and breathe. As you are taking in deep cleansing breaths, focus on the figures you see around you.

Good.

Notice the uniqueness of those who have come to you. Where are they standing? In what order have they revealed themselves to you? Pay attention to signals they are sharing. Do any of these signs seem familiar to you? Take in the features of every individual you see. How are they clothed? What sex, nationality, race, or origin do they represent? What color are their eyes or hair? What is the texture of their hair? Is it short, long, straight, or curly? Is it flowing or arranged in a specific manner? What catches your attention most about these beings? Do some stand out to you more than others and why? Can you notice any smells around you? Perhaps the scent of incense, oils, tobacco, or herbs? Are the individuals carrying items with them? Have they come bearing gifts or offerings for you? Can you sense anything that they may be saying to you? Are they showing glimpses or pictures of times that you may have shared with them? Do you hear specific words, messages, or names being spoken? Commune with those who have chosen to appear to you. Take a few more deep cleansing breaths while really focusing on all the questions involving those who are present.

Great.

Now, absorb the information you just received and thank your guides for showing themselves to you. You have just met a few of your spirit guides that are always present to guide, encourage, teach, and protect you along your soul journey. Thank Spirit for allowing this meeting to occur and then politely ask your guides to individually come forward to speak with you. Call upon your guides in whatever order you feel appropriate. One by one ask them what it is they are here to help you with. What is their purpose in your soul journey? Ask for their name or how they wish for you to call upon them. Ask to know what signs they will give that will help you to know that they are present. Ask anything that you feel may help better utilize their abilities for your higher good. Now, be still, listen, and wait patiently for their answers. You may notice that some guides give you more information than others. Trust Spirit and know that no matter how your guides respond it is in your best interest for your current position in your soul journey of life. As you continue to speak with your guides remember any gifts or special notions they present to you. While they exit, allowing for the next guide to enter, notice where they stand. Do they leave to your right or left while remaining in front of you? Do they go behind you positioned at your back to the right or left? Or do they exit completely disappearing back into the shadows around the bonfire waiting for you to call upon them as needed for a specific goal or time? Stop a minute and absorb all of these details.

Okay.

Now that you have shared intimate space and time with your guides, thank them once again for all the energy and guidance they imparted upon you. Let them know you request their help to fulfill your soul purpose and you will be open to continue to receive messages from them whenever they attempt to communicate. Bless them in returning to their sacred place. Watch as they retreat back into the shadows and smile as a sign of gratitude for partaking in such an enlightened spiritual experience.

Good.

Once you have said your good-byes and every guide has exited, return to your place by the fire. Acknowledge the atmosphere you first entered. Remember, you are again alone by the bonfire on an enchanted fall evening. As you close your eyes, begin to inhale the scents and warmth around you. Relax and breathe in preparation for your return from this journey.

Inhale, hold, one . . . two . . . three . . . now exhale. Begin slowly to come back to the present place and time.

Again, inhale, hold, one . . . two . . . three . . . now exhale. Now become aware of your body, how it is positioned, and start to move your arms, legs, hands, and feet.

Once more, inhale, hold, one . . . two . . . three . . . now exhale. When you are ready, slowly open your eyes and return to your original state.

JOURNAL SPACE

What colors or scents were present?

_____

_____

What sensations did you feel?

_____

_____

What messages did you see or hear?

_____

_____

Were you familiar with the place or any objects or people that were present?

_____

_____

What questions can you remember and answer from this meditation?

_____

_____

What caught your attention most during this journey?

_____

_____

What information would you most like to remember about this experience?

_____

_____

How can you apply information received from this experience to your current place in life?

_____

_____

What did you learn about yourself on this journey?

_____

_____

If there is one thing you could improve about your soul journey, starting today, what would that be?

_____

_____

What else would you like to remember about this experience?

_____

_____

Are there any unanswered questions or ideas sparked from this meditation that you would like to learn more about?

_____

_____

Continue writing about anything else special to you from this meditation.

_____

_____

CREATIVE ARTWORK SPACE

Past Life Meditation

Close your eyes and find a comfortable position. You may sit up with your feet flat on the floor or lie down. Whichever you prefer is great.

We are going to start by taking three deep breaths. Okay, let's begin.

Here we go, first breath. Inhale, hold, one . . . two . . . three . . . now exhale. Notice your face and shoulders start to relax.

Okay, again, inhale, hold, one . . . two . . . three . . . now exhale. Notice your legs and arms start to relax, and then your entire body.

One more time, inhale, hold, one . . . two . . . three . . . now exhale. The stresses of your day are melting away. You are now ready for the journey.

Imagine you are standing under a waterfall of pristine blue water. You can feel the mist of the water as it hits the rocks below. You can sense the strength of the water as it floods over the ledge above, rushing past your face, impacting the earth around you. The energy of the water is empowering, and the ground below your feet begins to tremble from the sheer force of life this atmosphere contains. While you stand under this wonderful creation of Mother Earth, you begin to feel your personal energy source become one with the water around you. As you take on the power and flow of the water, you catch yourself moving closer to the curtain of water in front of you. Nearing the rock ledge, you reach out your hands and are immediately overtaken by the water. You close your eyes and let go of all inhibitions as you are swept away under the weight of the flowing falls. Suddenly you are dropped into a pool of water and can sense the energy shift around you. The intensity of the downward flow of the waterfall has now turned into a methodical circular swirling energy. With every swirling wave, the water engulfs all stress, fear, doubt, and sadness you possess. You are overtaken with emotions of anticipation, happiness, hope, and love as your connectedness with Mother Earth grows stronger the longer you float in this pool of healing water. As peace takes over, you open your eyes for receiving what Spirit has for you. You know you have been brought here for a specific purpose, and you are ready to share in this experience. Take a minute and slowly embrace this pool of living water. Take a few deep breaths, open your eyes, and wait patiently as your reason for coming is slowly revealed.

Good.

Now, once your eyes are open, notice the white light and clouds surrounding you. In the midst of the clouds, scenes of past lives begin being played as if projected on a movie screen in front of you. Recall you are still floating in the pool of healing water now surrounded by Spirit's protective white light. Nothing you will see can harm you. This experience is simply a gift to be shared, in order for you to understand more clearly your higher purpose in your current soul journey. Now that Spirit has reinforced that you are safe and at peace, watch the scenes flashing before you, and note the era in which the past life is taking place. What details do you see that inform you of the time and space you once visited? Are there familiar faces around you? What roles are they playing in this particular life? What role are you playing in the scenes being shown? Are you rich, poor, a child or adult, male or female? Are you a teacher, healer, warrior, intuit, leader, or follower. Are you the tormenter or the tormented? Can you feel emotions tied to what you see with issues you deal with currently? Are situations from then revealing of certain fears or struggles you experience now? Were you kind and generous or selfish and stubborn? Did you understand love and compassion or struggle to connect with souls in this past life? Can you connect action from these scenes to reactions you exhibit now? Do you recognize how certain choices made then created karmic cycles you are finishing or starting now? Take a moment and really embrace, without judgment, all that is being shared with you. Absorb all that you can from what you are viewing. Try to connect energetically with choices made then in comparison to choices made now. What molded your decision making then in comparison to what drives your decision making now? What would you have done differently then that could have affected habits or life choices now?

Good.

Thank Spirit and ask for guidance and growth to occur as a result of viewing the scenes of your past lives or life. Some of you may have been shown numerous lives and others may have viewed scenes from one particular life. Either way trust that what was given was meant for your higher good. Ask Spirit what lessons you are to learn from this experience and what areas, values, relationships, or situations you need to reflect upon in order to heal and grow. Listen and notice if any words, messages, feelings, or pictures are shared with you. Be still and absorb all that is being offered to assist in your soul's evolvement.

Good.

Now, take a deep breath and realize once again that you are still floating in the pool of healing water. Take a moment and feel the water swirl around you. Notice the white light still radiating and consuming the space around you. Use this image as a reminder that Spirit is always with you, protecting and guiding you. While you look once more towards the clouds, notice they are starting to dissipate into the water around you. As each cloud is evaporated into the pool, the water begins to feel warm and full of life force energy. You sense the energy engulfing you. Relax. Let the water cover you, acting as a warm blanket of love. Embrace all the wonderful energy around you as you prepare to exit this journey.

Inhale, hold, one . . . two . . . three . . . now exhale. Begin slowly to come back to the present place and time.

Again, inhale, hold, one . . . two . . . three . . . now exhale. Now become aware of your body, how it is positioned, and start to move your arms, legs, hands, and feet.

Once more, inhale, hold, one . . . two . . . three . . . now exhale. When you are ready, slowly open your eyes and return to your original state.

JOURNAL SPACE

What colors or scents were present?

_____

_____

What sensations did you feel?

_____

_____

What messages did you see or hear?

_____

_____

Were you familiar with the place or any objects or people that were present?

_____

_____

What questions can you remember and answer from this meditation?

_____

_____

What caught your attention most during this journey?

_____

_____

What information would you most like to remember about this experience?

_____

_____

How can you apply information received from this experience to your current place in life?

_____

_____

_____

What did you learn about yourself on this journey?

_____

_____

_____

If there is one thing you could improve about your soul journey, starting today, what would that be?

_____

_____

_____

What else would you like to remember about this experience?

_____

_____

_____

Are there any unanswered questions or ideas sparked from this meditation that you would like to learn more about?

_____

_____

_____

Continue writing about anything else special to you from this meditation.

_____

_____

_____

CREATIVE ARTWORK SPACE

Connecting with the Other Side Meditation

Close your eyes and find a comfortable position. You may sit up with your feet flat on the floor or lie down. Whichever you prefer is great.

We are going to start by taking three deep breaths. Okay, let's begin.

Here we go, first breath. Inhale, hold, one . . . two . . . three . . . now exhale. Notice your face and shoulders start to relax.

Okay, again, inhale, hold, one . . . two . . . three . . . now exhale. Notice your legs and arms start to relax, and then your entire body.

One more time, inhale, hold, one . . . two . . . three . . . now exhale. The stresses of your day are melting away. You are now ready for the journey.

Think of a loved one who has crossed over that you would like to share this journey with. Next, envision something that connects you to this person. It can be a material object, perhaps an item they may have given you, or a personal belonging of theirs. It can be a picture of them or of a memory you shared together. Or you can create an image that connects you, such as a particular location, home, or environment you shared. Some of you may find that scents or nature, like rocks, sticks, or dirt, connects you. Whatever you choose, envision it now. Stare deep, deep, deep into the object or memory of choice. Once you have clearly envisioned this item or memory, surround this vision with white light. As you create a circle of white light, focus on making it brighter and bigger. Expand the circle as far as you choose around your item or memory. Put all of your energy and thoughts towards making the light as energetic as possible. As you project energy towards this light, notice the details of your created white light. Does the light sparkle? Is it cloudy or crystal clear? Is the light moving or stagnate? Are there other colors beginning to swirl amidst the white light? How does the light feel? Is it warm or cool? Does it tingle or vibrate as you project it around your special item or memory? Take a moment to absorb your vision and every detail related to what you have created.

Good.

Once you have encircled your vision with this amazing white light, call out to the loved one you chose to see. Ask them to come forward in whatever way possible and commune with you. Let the loved one you chose know you have created this circle of loving, protective white light for the two of you today and that, when they are ready, you would like them to enter the circle and share this journey. Once you have asked them to come forward, patiently wait, again staring into the center of your circle at the item or memory of choice. Continue to feed your white light with loving, positive energy. Be still. Watch and listen for anything that may be revealed to you.

Good.

Now, some of you may have noticed your loved one enter the circle right away in the form of a person or shadow. You may have seen features confirming their identity, or you may have instead had an intuitive sense of their presence. Some of your loved ones may have entered by showing themselves through glimpses of pictures. You may have heard or felt messages being shared and validated as they entered the circle. Some of you may have felt as if nothing at all presented itself. That's okay too. No matter what you received, continue to project energy towards the vision and light you created. Continue feeding your white light, creating balance and peace in your circle of energy. As you gain strength from this environment of love, so also will your loved one. This love will draw them to you, encouraging a visitation. If you're loved one has entered, please commune with them now. Send thoughts of healing, as you embrace their presence. Thank them for coming. Express your love for them however you choose. Any messages you hoped to share, do so now. Hug and bless them. Ask if they need your help with achieving growth on the other side. Ask any question that promotes the higher good of you both. Ask for signs that indicate when they are around so that you may more regularly commune with them. For those of you who felt as if no one appeared, you may notice that the energy and love projected from asking these questions allowed them to come through now. Take a moment to spend time receiving and sharing love, life, and energy with your loved one.

Great.

Now, while still focusing on your vision and white light, prepare to dismiss your loved one. Show gratitude for the visitations experienced today. Acknowledge that it takes a tremendous amount of energy and growth for them to appear. Thank Spirit for opening your higher consciousness so that you could receive them. Thank your loved one for this time and for the ability to connect. Tell them you will be open to future visitations in whatever manner they choose. Thank them for the protection, guidance, and love they shower upon you from the other side. Then send them away with all the love and light you can possibly fathom, allowing them to exit through the beautiful white light you created today.

Good.

Now, once your loved one has exited your circle of white light, focus on the item or memory of choice that connected you. Imagine putting this memory or item in a safe, sacred place where you can always recover it. After you have hidden away your item or memory, once again focus on your white circle of light. As you stare into the circle, begin to make it smaller, denser, and less bright. Shrink your light until it becomes a tiny ball of light. Then grab the ball and place it over your heart. While clenching the ball, absorb every memory created from this unforgettable experience into your heart space. Then take a deep breath and prepare to return from this journey.

Inhale, hold, one . . . two . . . three . . . now exhale. Begin slowly to come back to the present place and time.

Again, inhale, hold, one . . . two . . . three . . . now exhale. Now become aware of your body, how it is positioned, and start to move your arms, legs, hands, and feet.

Once more, inhale, hold, one . . . two . . . three . . . now exhale. When you are ready, slowly open your eyes and return to your original state.

JOURNAL SPACE

What colors or scents were present?

_____

_____

What sensations did you feel?

_____

_____

What messages did you see or hear?

_____

_____

Were you familiar with the place or any objects or people that were present?

_____

_____

What questions can you remember and answer from this meditation?

_____

_____

What caught your attention most during this journey?

_____

_____

What information would you most like to remember about this experience?

_____

_____

How can you apply information received from this experience to your current place in life?

_____

_____

What did you learn about yourself on this journey?

_____

_____

If there is one thing you could improve about your soul journey, starting today, what would that be?

_____

_____

What else would you like to remember about this experience?

_____

_____

Are there any unanswered questions or ideas sparked from this meditation that you would like to learn more about?

_____

_____

Continue writing about anything else special to you from this meditation.

_____

_____

CREATIVE ARTWORK SPACE

Unborn Child Meditation

Close your eyes and find a comfortable position. You may sit up with your feet flat on the floor or lie down. Whichever you prefer is great.

We are going to start by taking three deep breaths. Okay, Here we go, first breath. Inhale, hold, one . . . two . . . three . . . now exhale. Notice your face and shoulders start to relax.

Okay, again, inhale, hold, one . . . two . . . three . . . now exhale. Notice your legs and arms start to relax, and then your entire body.

One more time, inhale, hold, one . . . two . . . three . . . now exhale. The stresses of your day are melting away. You are now ready for the journey.

Envision yourself lying in a hammock between two large wise trees. The branches of the trees are hovering all around, and the foliage hanging from the branches gently brushes against your skin. A warm breeze of fresh air flows through the trees slowly rocking you side to side while you feel embraced by the strength of the hammock bed. You are completely relaxed and at ease. Your mind is open to receive all the universe wishes to share. Suddenly you are reminded of spring. A time of rebirth, growth, sprouting, and new beginnings. The sun is shining ever so brightly. You welcome the energy and warmth it offers while being protected and shielded by the massive trees holding you above the ground. You are completely connected with Mother Earth and the universe around you.

Good.

As you are continually rocked side to side, begin to picture the image of a young child being rocked and held close to its parent. Recognize the symbolism of the child being embraced and rocked with your place in the hammock. You know Spirit has brought you here for a reason. So, with that knowing, you slowly close your eyes and ask Spirit to reveal its sacred knowledge. Upon that request the image of the child becomes clearer. You can see vivid details of this precious little life. Take a moment and notice any distinguishing or familiar features. What color are the eyes, hair, and skin? Is the child male or female? Is there more than one child present? Touch the child's adorable little nose and count each finger and toe. Relax and enjoy the memories of this experience. Welcome the warmth and softness of this new creation into your world. Notice the scent of the child as you embrace them and breathe in the purity of life around you. Soak up every detail of this experience. Pay attention for any words, names, messages, or images being shared during this engagement with new life. Be still and listen. Just wait for this child to share everything it has to offer. Now, burn the details of this experience into a sacred place in your heart and memory. Thank Spirit for this invitation and smile, for you have just met your unborn child. Hug your child and let them know you are excited to have been chosen as their parent and allow the child to exit to its waiting place until you can be reunited.

Good.

As your child's image slowly disappears you will remember you are still lying in your hammock. Take in the peacefulness of your surroundings once more. Bask in the warmth of the sun. Feel the foliage of the aged, strong trees brushing against your skin. Inhale the fresh air and embrace the breeze as it rocks you side to side, side to side until slowly it begins to subside. As your hammock stops, take a deep breath and wait to return from your journey.

Inhale, hold, one . . . two . . . three . . . now exhale. Begin slowly to come back to the present place and time.

Again, inhale, hold, one . . . two . . . three . . . now exhale. Now become aware of your body, how it is positioned, and start to move your arms, legs, hands, and feet.

Once more, inhale, hold, one . . . two . . . three . . . now exhale. When you are ready, slowly open your eyes and return to your original state.

JOURNAL SPACE

What colors or scents were present?

_____

_____

What sensations did you feel?

_____

_____

What messages did you see or hear?

_____

_____

Were you familiar with the place or any objects or people that were present?

_____

_____

What questions can you remember and answer from this meditation?

_____

_____

What caught your attention most during this journey?

_____

_____

What information would you most like to remember about this experience?

_____

_____

How can you apply information received from this experience to your current place in life?

_____

_____

What did you learn about yourself on this journey?

_____

_____

If there is one thing you could improve about your soul journey, starting today, what would that be?

_____

_____

What else would you like to remember about this experience?

_____

_____

Are there any unanswered questions or ideas sparked from this meditation that you would like to learn more about?

_____

_____

Continue writing about anything else special to you from this meditation.

_____

_____

CREATIVE ARTWORK SPACE

Symbolism

The next section is meant as a brief, fun glossary of the symbolism of some of my favorite flowers, trees, animals, and stones/crystals. I have included both common and uncommon varieties of each category, some of which are the personal spirit guides, totems, or sources that I feel most closely connected to. I hope you find in the glossary below some of the flowers, trees, animals, and stones/crystals you encountered in your meditations. I highly encourage you to take the information you received from completing this book and extend your knowledge by taking a shamanic journey with someone in your area or by reading some of the wonderful references I have provided at the end of this book. Review the information you wrote in your journal, and learn as much as you can about the symbolism of the flowers, trees, animals, and stones that appeared in your meditation.

Flowers

Calla lily: Deep knowledge, intuition, catching dreams

Cherry Blossom: Abundance, new beginnings (new romance or new energies)

Daffodil: New beginnings, leaving past behind, celebration of being alive, regeneration

Daisy: Happiness, a positive outlook, appreciating the simple things, discernment of others

Dandelion: Magic, wishes coming true, creating your own desires

Lotus: Enlightenment, growing amidst unfavorable conditions

Rosebud: Anticipation for what's to come, opening your heart/spirit to unlimited potential and dreams, fulfillment of desires

Sunflower: Follower of the "light," connection to divine rays of energy, healing energy, eternal hope, blessing of nourishment

Tulip: Love will not pass by you, living in the moment, enjoying and embracing life

Venus Flytrap: Preparation meets opportunity for reward, patience yields reward, knowing you're in the right place at the right time, at the destined moment reward can be delivered instantly

Water lily: Rising above struggles, great hope, courage to do anything, aligning with higher self, opening to receive guidance from above

Stones/Crystals

Amber: Healing, calming, balance, clairvoyance, spiritual wisdom, joy, happiness, self-confidence, courage, respect

Amethyst: Facilitates change, transforms negativity, awakens higher consciousness and wisdom, clairsentience

Aventurine: Leadership, decisiveness, compassion, empathy, perseverance, enhances creativity, regeneration of the heart, brings serenity, clairsentience

Citrine: Manifestation, prosperity, abundance, joy, clarity, removes blockages, creates heart's desire

Emerald: Renewal of infinite spirit, creative powers and abundance, healing the heart, bringing freshness and vitality to the spirit, inspiration, infinite patience, unity, compassion, unconditional love, the promotion of friendship, balance between partners, domestic bliss, contentment, loyalty, security in love, vision, intuition, clairvoyance, revealing one's truths, intelligence with discernment

Labradorite: Healing, understanding of auras, facilitates one's receptivity to prophecy, foretelling, psychic abilities

Moonstone: Increases feminine energy and fertility, provides goddess energy, promotes intuition, provides protection, increases success, adds to internal reflection of self, enhances psychic abilities

Obsidian: Provides protection from negative energies so others cannot penetrate your space, grounding, discharges negative tensions, offers psychic protection, brings focus

Pink Tourmaline: Opens heart to pure love and healing, nurturing, balances emotions and mood, brings back passion

Smoky Quartz: Grounding, anchoring, psychic protection, transmutes energies, enhances mystical forces

Tiger's eye: Healing, balances and creates harmony between energies, helps you go with the flow, helps release fears and anxiety, increases discernment in decision making, improves self-confidence, provides strength, enhances creativity

Trees

Aspen: Healing properties, protection from unwanted spirits, release of old fears, the strength to face fear that comes with the unknown as you move forward, listening to self and believing in your own abilities, understanding that love overcomes all things, finding true joy, releasing our old habits of self-criticism and guilt

Bonsai: Meditation, a sense of harmony, peace, balance, and connectedness to life and nature, staying strong through hardship, acknowledging beauty in all things

Elm: Inner strength, intuition, psychic abilities, instinct over conscious decision making, family, tradition, grounding, devotion, loyalty, outlasting the weaker individuals in society even when faced with defeat, warrior and goddess energies

Fig: Fulfillment of aspirations and dreams, good works, kindness, healing, spiritual nourishment

Lemon: Cleansing, energizing, healing, refreshment, new energies present, clarity, drawing in of spirit guides, longevity, clever usages of adversity, ritual use for attraction of love and partnership

Oak: Courage, power, healing, strength in unfavorable conditions, protection, justice, honesty, nobility, youthfulness, fertility, good fortune, manifestation, wisdom, spirit realms

Olive: Peace, strength in adversity, healing, rewarding of victory, fruitfulness, regeneration, promotion of health and well-being, abundance, wisdom, glory, fertility, pureness

Ponderosa Pine: Inspiration to rise above difficulties and persist against the odds, the way to success is inner peace and strength, calmness, serenity, humbleness, good fortune, prosperity, a sign of fertility, birthing, protection, vitality, resistance, vigor, determination, strength, rejuvenation, refreshment of body and spirit, purification, cleansing of sacred space and ritual objects, dispelling of negative energy, crystal cleansing, understanding consciousness, manifestation

Walnut: Awakening of abundance and prosperity, fertility, wisdom, rebirth, secret knowledge, clarity about what goes on around you, initiation of creative energies that allow you to follow your own path

Willow: Creativity, fertility, female rites of passage, inspiration, emotion, binding love, protection, healing, immortality, flexibility to bend around obstacles, creation of desires, expression of emotions, opening to subconscious, clairvoyance

Animals

Billy goat: Spiritual ambitions, time for new heights of aspirations and new endeavors, success and wealth, strong work ethic for achieving goals, having faith in personal abilities and strengths

Cheetah: Energies moving with great speed, remaining focused on your goal of chasing dreams, flexibility and need for revisions in order to attain your goal, clear intentions with creations, great empathy for others, fearlessness, responding quickly and instantly, enjoying solitude but understanding purpose of connectedness with others when needed

Chipmunk: Something good that delights your heart is on its way, artistic qualities, intuition, playfulness, seeing what is right in front of you even though others may miss it, claircognizance

Eagle: Spiritual protection, carrying prayers, bringing strength, courage, wisdom, healing, creation, ability to see hidden spiritual truths, rising above the material to see the spiritual, connection to spirit guides and teachers, great power, balance, dignity with grace, a connection with higher truths, intuition, creative spirit achieved through knowledge and hard work

Fox: Guidance for swiftly finding your way around obstacles, quick thinking and adaptability, guidance when facing tricky situations, physical or mental responsiveness, increased awareness, seeing through deception, a call to be discerning, ability to find your way around, dream work

Frog: Time to find opportunities in transition, fertility, abundance, good luck in having a happy family, easily swimming through tough life transitions, assurance while traveling, working to enhance your intuition and strengthen your connection with the spirit world

Giraffe: Elongating your vision, stretching yourselves and reaching as far as you can, acknowledging your remarkable potential to rise to a challenge, maintaining grace and balance through challenges, communication, expression, vision, third eye intuition

Gorilla: Leadership, management of others with compassion, dignity, inner strength, decisiveness, protective of those around you, strength of community

Grey wolf: Adapting to energy shifts, leading with intuition, telepathy, evolving, assessing and adapting to situations, deep awareness and perception, protection of pack/family, facing fears that hold you back from achieving your greatest destiny, discipline, freedom, discernment in knowing what is best for you to avoid

Horse: Fierce competitor, endurance, freedom, strength, confidence, the mystical charm that draws others in, telepathy, a deep sense of knowing, heading toward destiny, warrior energy, and energy needed to discover your life partner or mate, alpha energy, companionship, serenity

Lion: Letting go of stress, strong family ties, strength, courage, energy, self-fulfillment, feminine energy, cooperation, community, creativity, intuition, imagination, soul rising to surface, power, wealth, passion, affection, serenity unless provoked, working with others while maintaining your own individuality

Owl: Seeing what others miss, remaining still amidst noise of life, discernment of others' motives, connection with inner voice, trusting instincts especially about others, clairvoyance, knowledge, piercing through darkness to reach your happiness, vision, protection, transition, silent wisdom

Rabbit: Abundance, comfort, vulnerability, fertility, new life, new beginnings, sentiment, desire, procreation of life and ideas, a time of rebirth, promise of wonderful things to come, longevity, creativity, harmony, family and community, increased perception, external knowledge, health, ability to analyze and break down concepts or issues, groundedness, deep emotion, reflection, being highly sensitive and alert, reminding us to utilize tools we have within ourselves

Red-tailed hawk: Clear-sightedness, being observant, enhanced long term memory, messages from the universe, guardianship, recalling past lives, courage, wisdom, illumination, seeing the bigger picture, creativity, truth, life experience, wise use of opportunities, overcoming problems, focus, higher expression of psychic abilities and vision, paying attention to subtle messages and underlying truths, intensity of energy, kundalini life force, ability to move between seen and unseen worlds, focus on soul destiny, promoting spiritual growth, rewards reaped outweigh the burden of hard work

Skunk: Opportunity to become more confident in your interactions with others, ability to meet life's challenges with a calm and peaceful heart, having the respect you require to get to where you wish to be, walking your talk in order to set an example for others, respecting yourself and your own beliefs, having the courage and willpower to right a wrong, justice, a reputation of calm confidence precedes you, being gentle yet powerful, assertiveness without ego, being charismatic, avoiding conflict but maintaining self-respect, speaking your truth always, not suppressing your emotions so to avoid exploding

Snake: Negative and positive duality, rebirth, renewal, new beginnings, releasing or shedding of old thoughts or ways, acceptance of inner knowing without guilt or others' judgments affecting you, kundalini life force, enlightenment, healing, opportunities, transition and change are manifesting, guidance physically and spiritually, sensitivity to healing yourself and healing coming from others, cultivating energy from connectedness with nature and earth

Turtle: Walking our path in peace and sticking to it with determination and serenity, reminding you to slow down and take a break in your busy life to find more grounded and long-lasting solutions, cultivating peace of mind or a peaceful relationship with the environment, being grounded even in moments of disturbances and chaos, pacing yourself, persistence, emotional strength, understanding, ancient wisdom, spirit of the water, being fluid with nature of emotions

Explanation of Metaphysical Terms Used in This Book

I wanted to share some basic metaphysical concepts and terms with you as a fun reference for helping you connect with ideas shared throughout the meditations in this book. My descriptions are very vague and by no means are the answer to all the complexity of the metaphysical world. I have shared some of my favorite ideas and fun facts, as well as added a few explanations of some ideas to better clarify their usage in this book.

Description of the Metaphysical Senses

There are four main metaphysical senses described as clairaudience, claircognizance, clairsentience, and clairvoyance. These senses are used as mechanisms for connecting with and receiving messages from higher sources of Spirit. The entities attributed to these messages are often thought of as one's soul, spirit guides, decease loved ones, disincarnate beings, or angels.

The "clair" senses allow us to receive messages of divine guidance for both our higher good and that of others. As you may have noticed I asked you throughout the meditations to listen, feel, sense, taste, smell, and/or touch as part of your journey. The "clair" senses are the expression, in metaphysical terms, of the gifts you were asked to draw upon while completing this journal. If you have just become aware of the "clairs" while doing the meditations in this book, you can now reflect upon the senses you were most connected with and as a result will have an avenue by which to explore and develop your abilities.

Clairaudience

"Clairaudience" means "clear hearing by mental information being received." It is the ability to hear messages from Spirit in thought. Thoughts come in the form of repetitious words, phrases, or ideas. You may mentally hear answers to questions like a calm, clear voice that always speaks with complete logic. Sometimes the messages are clear, other times muffled. When repetitive thoughts continually enter your head, even when you are not consciously thinking about them, you are experiencing clairaudience. Telepathic communication is another form of clairaudience, in which you can tune into another person's thoughts. This can be done in the presence of the person or remotely, provided both parties are open. This often happens naturally over time with people who are very close to you.

Claircognizance

"Claircognizance" means "clear knowing or thinking." It is a metaphysical sense of positive knowing, even if it may go against everything others tell you about a situation. Claircognizance can be in the form of finishing other people's sentences because you know the answer before they finish the thought, or you may find yourself knowing immediately if someone is lying to you, even though you have no evidence to back up your thought. Clear thinking is present when information randomly pops into your head that you know is correct. It can come in the form of predictions, premonitions, or as a feeling of certainty. You may have knowledge of places, events, situations, or people without having received the information in a traditional manner. It may come across as a sense of déjà vu. Many times you will "know" the answer but be unable to back up your statement or explain how. Many people have this ability and explain it as a "gut feeling." However, many doubt their own claircognizant abilities, especially if they require validation or fear their "knowing" will be discounted by others who are not receptive to the information or the way that it was received.

Clairsentience

"Clairsentience" mean "clear feeling" recurring physically or emotionally. Clairsentience is active when physical or emotional feelings suddenly wash over you with no apparent connection to your current state of mind. You may suddenly feel sad or extremely anxious for no reason. You may feel the need to cancel plans at the last minute or opt out of continuing a certain path or direction. With clairsentience, you may feel an unexplained sense of foreboding or experience physical symptoms that are not your own. Unexplained stomachaches, sweaty palms, instant anger, tingling, or feeling generally sick are quite common. These physical and emotion symptoms are indications of messages being communicated to change your plans or course of action. By embracing these messages, this metaphysical sense can help you to prepare and protect yourself from energetic situations or people that may not be in your best interest.

Clairvoyance

"Clairvoyance" means "clear seeing of mental images within your third eye about an object, person, location or physical event." It is known as your sixth sense or spiritual sight. With this metaphysical sense you have visions or visual flashes while awake, in dreams, or other relaxed states. Clairvoyance also includes noticing auras, energy fields, colors, or symbols surrounding a person. You may mentally see visuals of loved ones who have crossed or images of spirit guides and other ascended entities when they are trying to communicate. Clairvoyance also allows you to receive visuals of words in regards to questions or messages for yourself or others.

Other "Clairs"

Clairalience

"Clairalience" means "clear smelling." It can be subcategorized under any of the main metaphysical senses. For example you may smell the scent of your grandmother's perfume before clairsentience allows you to feel her nearby. In this situation clairalience provided validation that your grandmother was in fact the person present.

Clairambience

"Clairambience" means "clear tasting." It too can be subcategorized under any of the four main "clairs." An example of clairambience would be tasting blood before claircognizance allows you to know someone passed from a trauma.

Clairalience and Clairambience are not mentioned as often as the four main metaphysical senses, but are relevant for most intuits. These senses act as supportive aids for heightening the receptiveness of the other metaphysical senses. The experience of smelling or tasting usually occurs when Spirit is trying to communicate a connection with an event or person related to a message being received. Despite more predominately experiencing clairvoyance, clairaudience, clairsentience, or claircognizance, in adjunction with those, you will at times also need clairalience and clairambience sensations as validation for the messages received through the four main metaphysical senses.

Chakras Simplified

Chakras are vital energy centers within our body that spiral together to aid in healing. There are seven main chakras that correlate with seven colors from the spectrum. Recognizing these powerful energy centers stems from ancient Eastern medicine beliefs. When the chakras are balanced, clear, and free flowing, your body is able to heal itself both spiritually and physically. Below is a simplified version of the descriptions of the chakra system. For more detailed information, I highly recommend reading, taking related classes, and experiencing Reiki treatments in your local area. Understanding the connection of emotional and physical energy as it relates to overall health will be life changing for you.

Base/Root Chakra—Red

Sacral Chakra—Orange

Solar Plexus Chakra—Yellow

Heart Chakra—Green/Pink

Throat Chakra—Blue

Brow/Third Eye Chakra—Indigo

Crown Chakra—Purple/White

Credits and Great Reads

Books:

Andrews, Ted. *Animal Speaks*. Woodbury, Minnesota: Llewellyn Publications, 2010.

Edwards, John. *Infinite Quest*. New York, New York: Sterling Ethos, 2010.

Lembo, Margaret Ann. *Color Your Life With Crystals: Your First Guide to Crystals, Colors and Chakras*. Forres, Scotland: Earthdancer Books GmbH, 2013.

Lembo, Margaret Ann. *Chakra Awakening*. Woodbury, Minnesota: Llewellyn Publications, 2011.

Websites:

http://www.TheGoddessTree.com/

http://www.SpiritAnimal.Info/

http://www.UniverseofSymbolism.com/

http://Spirit-Animals.com/

Hi, my name is Paige. I reside in Colorado with my beautiful family consisting of my Love Justin, our insightful son, our inquisitive two daughters, and our goddess kitty. Life is busy, but I would not change a thing. My house is always full of energy and life. There is never a dull moment. In my spare time, if there is such a thing, I love to enjoy everything Colorado has to offer, from hiking and camping in the spring and summer to, of course, skiing in the winter. I thrive off the energy that vibrates from the earth of this magnificent state. There is no other place for me to call home. I have worn many hats throughout the years. My first career was as a dental hygienist. After eleven years of hygiene and multiple babies, I decided to stay at home. Then I began the journey of being a stay-at-home mommy. During this time I was finally able to delve into passions I have had for years but never found time to pursue. I started completing certifications in several different realms of the metaphysical world such as Psychic Training, Reiki energy healing, and many other courses that taught me to develop the intuitive abilities that I was born with. I currently own the business Serene Escapes & Healing (www.SereneEscapesHealing.com) and blog at www.MetaphysicalMommies.com. I am a practicing Psychic Medium/Intuitive Guide providing guidance and love to those who need help in improving, and evolving in, their soul journey of this life. I am constantly re-discovering my own identity and can't wait to see, from day to day, what Spirit will inspire me to pursue or offer next as part of my business. In addition to the world of metaphysics, I have always loved to write and have known it was a calling of mine to share my thoughts with others. Although I have written my whole life, this book is officially my first published piece of art. I hope you enjoy it and look forward to many more.

Audio Download Page

Please visit: www.SereneEscapesHealing.com/Books-by-Paige.
Click on Book: *My Spiritual Journal of Guided Meditations* and
follow instructions to register and download accompanying
audio for the book.

Audio Download Page

Please visit: www.SereneEscapesHealing.com/Books-by-Paige.
Click on Book: *My Spiritual Journal of Guided Meditations* and
follow instructions to register and download accompanying
audio for the book.

www.ingramcontent.com/pod-product-compliance
Lightning Source LLC
Chambersburg PA
CBHW050449110726
47899CB00003B/874